ICKY · RICKY · 4

THE HOLE TO CHINA

Written & illustrated by

MICHAEL REX

A STEPPING STONE BOOK™

Random House 🏠 New York

To Rick W., the Real Icky Ricky

Copyright © 2014 by Michael Rex

All rights reserved. Published in the United States by Random House Children's Books, a division of Random House LLC, a Penguin Random House Company, New York.

Random House and the colophon are registered trademarks and A Stepping Stone Book and the colophon are trademarks of Random House LLC.

Visit us on the Web!
SteppingStonesBooks.com
randomhouse.com/kids

Educators and librarians, for a variety of teaching tools, visit us at RHTeachersLibrarians.com

Library of Congress Cataloging-in-Publication Data
Rex, Michael, author, illustrator.
The hole to China / written and illustrated by Michael Rex.
p. cm. — (Icky Ricky ; #4)
"A Stepping Stone Book."
Summary: "He's digging a hole to China, in his backyard. He found a free toilet in someone's garbage. He fell into a pigpen with a muddy mega-pig. Icky Ricky is up to his eyeballs in trouble—and ick." —Provided by publisher.
ISBN 978-0-385-37556-6 (pbk.) — ISBN 978-0-385-37557-3 (lib. bdg.) — ISBN 978-0-385-37558-0 (ebook)
[1. Behavior—Fiction. 2. Humorous stories.] I. Title.
PZ7.R32875Ho 2014 [E]—dc23 2013048840

Printed in the United States of America

10 9 8 7 6 5 4 3 2 1

This book has been officially leveled by the F&P Text Level Gradient™ Leveling System.

Random House Children's Books supports the First Amendment and celebrates the right to read.

CONTENTS

"Ricky! Gus! Stew!" shouted Gus's dad over the loud rain. "What the heck are you doing in that hole?"

"Having a sleepover," said Gus. "What are *you* doing here?"

"I brought your toothbrush. You forgot it!" said Gus's dad. "But why are you having a sleepover in a muddy hole in Ricky's yard?"

"Because we didn't want to go to the Island of Zombie Babies!" said Ricky.

"What?" said Gus's dad. "Just tell me what's going on!"

"All right," said Ricky. . . .

It all started this morning. I had decided to dig a hole to China in my backyard. It was something I'd always wanted to do, and I thought today would be a good day to do it.

Gus and Stew came over to remind me that tonight was Heavy-Trash Night. That's when everyone in town puts out big things the garbage truck won't normally take.

Gus was like, "What are you doing?"

I told them I was digging a hole to China.

Stew said, "You know that's impossible. There's a giant wad of burning magma at the center of the earth."

Then I said, "Yeah, duh. That's why my tunnel isn't going to go straight. It's going to be curved and stuff."

Gus said, "Hey. Maybe it could stop at other places. Like England, or Japan, or Cleveland."

Then Stew said, "Or maybe Guam."

Gus and I started laughing. I asked, "Guam? What's Guam?"

Stew told us that Guam was a tiny island way out in the Pacific Ocean.

"It might be really hard to make a tunnel to a little island," I said. "If you don't come up at the right place, you could come up under the ocean."

"Or end up at the wrong island," said Stew.

Gus was like, "Yeah, a creepy deserted island."

Then I said, "With zombie babies."

All at once we said, "The Island of Zombie Babies! Jinx!" We started laughing.

I shouted, "Island of Zombie Babies, here we come!"

Gus and Stew jumped into the hole and
started digging with me.

Then I asked, "What are we going to do
when we get to the Island of Zombie Babies?"

Stew said, "I guess we'll have to fight
them."

"Yeah, and there would probably be hundreds. Maybe thousands," said Gus.

I scratched my head and asked, "What's the point of going there?"

"It sounds like a lot of work," said Gus.

"Maybe it's not a great idea," said Stew. "Let's go to Guam!"

We dug all day. My mom even brought us lunch outside. We dug and dug until we made a pretty great hole. It was so deep that if we stood in it, we could hardly see out.

"You know," I said, "I don't think we're ever gonna get to Guam. But, man, this is a really cool hole."

"I think it's the best hole ever," said Stew. He sat down. "Ugh. I can't dig anymore."

I got down with him. "Yeah. I'm beat," I said. "That was some serious digging."

Gus sat, too. It was crowded. The dirt was cool, and we just sort of hung out there awhile.

"This is a pretty good place to chill," said Gus.

"I wish we could sleep here," said Stew. "Like a hotel."

"Yes!" I said. Then I had my best idea of the day. "Let's make it a Hole-tel!"

"We need to decorate it!" Stew said.

All at once we shouted, "Heavy-Trash Night!" We all jumped up and climbed out of the hole.

We grabbed my dad's hand truck from the garage and ran down the street. At first we didn't see anything good. There were just a couple of old flowerpots, a busted door, two soggy rugs, and a box full of boxes. Really. It was just a big box filled with little boxes. It was weird.

We went around the next corner,
and then we saw the greatest thing ever!
A toilet!

Next to the toilet we found the other
best thing ever, a little kid's mattress! There
was a painting, too. It was of a duck. We
grabbed all three things. The toilet was
heavy, but we got it on the hand truck. Gus
carried the little mattress, and Stew carried
the painting.

"These are going to look great in the Hole-tel," I said.

We got back to my house. We were going to try to carry the toilet down into the hole, but it was too heavy.

"Should we just drop it?" asked Stew.

"It might break," said Gus.

Then I had the best idea ever.

I took the little mattress and wrapped it around the toilet.

"See?" I said. "It's padded now. Like in a moving truck."

We pushed it to the edge of the hole, and I said, "On the count of three . . ."

We never wait for three. We dropped the toilet down into the hole. And you know what? Only that lid piece in the back broke.

We flattened out the mattress and hung the duck picture on the side of the hole. It looked awesome. It was getting dark, so we all went home for dinner.

Later, Gus and Stew came back for a
sleepover in the Hole-tel. I had made a sign
that they thought was really awesome.

We all had sleeping bags. We took
them down into the hole and tried to get
comfortable. We were really tired because
we had been digging all day. But there

wasn't any room to sleep. We tried to sleep standing up. That didn't work. We tried to sleep on top of each other. That didn't work. I tried sleeping on the toilet. That totally didn't work.

"I have to use the toilet," said Gus.

"No way," said Stew. "It's not a real toilet."

"Then what's the point of it?" asked Gus.

"Because no one's going to stay in a hotel without a toilet," I said.

Stew and I both said, "Duh."

We all started laughing at how stupid that conversation was. Then *boom!* There was some thunder and lightning, and it started to rain.

First we just threw our sleeping bags over our heads, but the hole was filling up fast with water. We tried to climb out, but since it was all muddy we couldn't. We tried standing on the toilet, but we still had nothing to grab. That's when you found us.

"Well," said Gus's dad, "I guess that makes perfect sense if you're a ten-year-old boy. But I think it's nuts! C'mon, it's pouring. Let's get you out of there." He reached into the hole and pulled Gus up, then Ricky, and then Stew.

Then he slipped and fell into the hole. He lay for a moment in the giant puddle at the bottom.

"You know, you're going to have to start charging more money for this Hole-tel," he said.

"Why?" said Ricky.

"Because," said Gus's dad, "it has a pool now!"

RICKY'S
ARCHAEOLOGY

#1: My Bedroom Closet

I like to dig, so I really like archaeology.
What's cool about archaeology is that it
shows us how people lived in the past.
Digging through the layers in my bedroom
closet allows me to relive my own history.

#1: My woodworking period
(Saws, glue, sawdust, sandpaper)

#2: My pastry chef period
(Flour, bowls, sugar, blueberries)

#3: My collecting period
(Rocks, soda cans, pizza crusts, long ropes)

#4: My sandwich period
(Bread, peanut butter, mayonnaise, special sauce)

#5: My beach-in-a-closet period
(Sand, shells, a plastic bag filled with salt water,
crabs)

#6: My every-single-sock-I-have-ever-worn period
(Sport, dress, casual, solid, striped)

#7: Floor/backpack from third grade

"Look out!" Ricky called as he ran from the front door of Stew's house. He plowed right into Stew, who was walking in.

"Oomph!" said Stew. The boys toppled over each other and down the front steps.

"Why are you in our house?" asked Stew's mom, who was right behind Stew. "And why are you wearing a dress?"

"Because the Goofenhausers lost their dog!"

Stew laughed. "The Goofen-whos?"

"The Goofenhausers! They're really nice!" said Ricky.

"Ricky," said Stew's mom, "you're not making any sense!"

"Okay! Okay!" said Ricky as he was getting up. . . .

It all started when I was walking down the street today. I saw this flyer for a lost dog. There were lots of flyers, so I took one down and brought it over to show Stew. When I got here, Stella was sitting on the front steps.

"Hey," I said. "Is Stew here? There's a lost dog that we should go look for."

"No," said Stella. "He went to the dentist with my mom."

"Oh," I said. "Do you want to go look for the dog?"

She said no.

"Listen to this," I said, and I read the flyer. " 'Lost dog. Answers to Roxy. Last seen on the corner of Driggs and Bayard. She's a really sweet dog, and we miss her so much. It would mean the world to us to have her home again. Thanks, Mr. and Mrs. Goofenhauser.' "

Stella didn't seem that interested.

"And look, there's a picture of the dog and her owners. See?" I showed her the picture. "We should try to help them."

"No," said Stella. I thought she was acting kind of weird, because usually she would have helped look for a lost dog.

"These people really want their dog back," I said.

"So what? I've got my own problems," said Stella.

All of a sudden, this strange moaning came from the house! Stella screamed and put her hands over her ears.

"What the heck is that?" I asked.

"It's a ghost or a demon or something!" said Stella. "The house is possessed. That's why I'm out here and not inside."

I was like, "Awesome! Let's go find it! I've always wanted to hunt a ghost." I tried to go into the house.

"No!" she said. "I'm not allowed to have boys over when Mom's not home."

"Well, then I'll pretend I'm a girl. Let me wear some of your clothes," I said.

"That's stupid," she said. "You'll still look like a boy."

"C'mon," I said. I stepped past her, into the doorway. The moaning started again. We both screamed. We ran into the house, ran up to her room, jumped on her bed, and hid under a blanket.

"No boys under the blanket!" she said, and kicked me hard. I fell off the bed and banged my head on a bookshelf.

"Quiet!" she said. I stayed on the ground for a moment till everything got calm again.

"Put this on," said Stella. She handed me a princess-type dress.

"Hey," I said, "this is an old Halloween costume or something."

"I don't want you to ruin my real clothes," said Stella. "You get everything filthy."

I put on the dress. She told me to sit down and started putting makeup on my face. There were brushes and pencils and lip stuff, and it was all kind of yucky. Now, I don't mind getting messy, but this was different. She put a wig on me, too. She held up a mirror.

"Yeah," said Stella. "It looks like you fell out of the ugly tree and hit every branch on the way down!"

The moaning started again. Stella covered her ears. The moans weren't as loud upstairs.

"Let's go find it," I said. We stepped into the hall. I wanted to look in Stew's room, but there was a sign on the door:

A sign under that said:

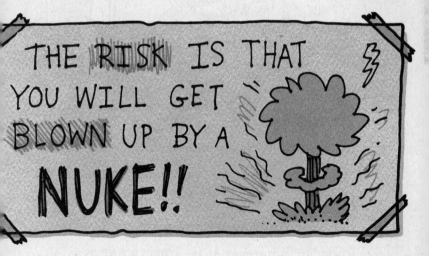

They were awesome signs.

I'd been in Stew's house a lot, so I knew where things were.

"Let's look in the attic first," I said.

"No way," said Stella. "I don't even like going up there on a normal day."

I turned the knob to the attic door. It wouldn't open.

"Mom keeps it locked now," said Stella, "ever since you and Stew tried to turn it into a dance club and flooded it with soap bubbles. Anyway, I don't want to find the ghost or whatever it is. I just want it to go away."

"If we want it to go away, we have to have a séance," I said.

"What's that?" asked Stella.

"It's when you talk to a ghost. You can ask it to leave or do something," I said.

"Let's ask it to leave," said Stella.

"Sure," I said. We went downstairs and sat on the living room floor.

"Sit across from me," I said.

Stella sat down. I crossed my legs. Stella crossed her legs, too. I reached out my hands.

"Hold my hands," I said.

"No way! You're disgusting," she said.

"Well, then it won't work," I said.

The moaning started again, and Stella screamed. She got up, ran to the kitchen, and came back wearing big dishwashing gloves. She grabbed my hands.

"Tell the ghost to leave," she said.

"Okay, okay!" I said. I closed my eyes and said, "Spirit of this house . . . can you hear me?"

There was no response. Nothing. Everything was quiet. I tried again.

"Spirit of this house," I said in my most serious voice, "my name is Ricky."

"You're a girl, remember?" said Stella.

"Oh. Right!" I said. I did my best girl voice.

"That's not a real name," said Stella.

"What name would you use?" I asked.

"Well, since you're the world's ugliest girl, your name should be Uglina Grossella," said Stella. She's as good at making up names as Stew is.

"Is Grossella a last name or a middle name?" I asked.

"Middle," she said.

"Then my full name is Uglina Grossella Hotwings," I said. I cracked up.

Stella finally started laughing, but just a little bit. "Boys think the stupidest things are funny," she said.

I grabbed her hands and talked to the ghost again.

"O spirit of the house, my name is Uglina," I said. "Can you hear me?" Everything was quiet. "If you hear me, give us a sign."

Nothing. It was silent. Then I farted. I really let one rip.

"Ugggh!" said Stella. "Why are boys so gross?" She held her nose.

"How dare you call Uglina Grossella
Hotwings a boy?" I said in my girlie voice.
Stella shoved me, and I fell back and
bonked my head on the wall.

WHAM!

A picture of an old lady fell off the wall into my lap.

"Grandma!" said Stella. She grabbed the picture.

"Your grandma's trying to contact you!" I said.

TO BE CONTINUED . . .

"Ricky!" called Ricky's dad as he carefully walked down the dark street. "Why are you out here in the dark, all dressed in black? Are you guys supposed to be ninjas or something?"

Ricky and Stew were standing in front of Gus's house.

"No. Special Ops," said Ricky.

"That makes total sense," said Ricky's dad as he rolled his eyes. "Why the heck are you dressed as Special Ops?"

"Because Gus's mom won't let him eat junk food," said Ricky.

"Soldier!" said Ricky's dad. "Explain yourself, right now!"

Ricky stood at attention.

YESSIR!

It all started when we went over to
Gus's house to see if he wanted to go bike
riding or something. His mom told us that
he was really sick and had to stay home.
I asked if we could see him. She said it
wasn't a good idea, because she didn't want
us to get sick, too.

As we left his house, a paper airplane
came flying out of the window of Gus's
room. It had writing on the wings that said,
"Don't let my mom see you with this." So
I stuck it under my shirt, and we headed
down the street.

When we were sure that Gus's mom couldn't see us, we stopped and unfolded the paper airplane. Gus had written more on the inside. It said, "Help! My mom is making me eat only healthy junk for the next few days. Can you guys get me some real food? You know what I like. I will look for you when it gets dark. Make sure my mom doesn't catch you." There was a twenty-dollar bill taped onto the plane. "Here is my birthday money. Don't spend it all."

We rode our bikes downtown to the supermarket to get the food for Gus.

"What should we buy?" asked Stew.

"I think we should get these! Gus loves them," I said.

"He likes it when his fingers get all yellow," said Stew. "He says that his hands are lava and if he touches you you'll melt!"

"We should get these!" I said, and I

held up a bag of his favorite cookies. "He only eats Chips-a-Plenty."

Stew was like, "Sweet!"

We were looking around for something else.

Stew held up a box of taco shells. "What about these?"

I was like, "Nah."

Then I held up a can of spaghetti shaped like prehistoric animals.

Stew said, "Nah."

Then we went around the corner to

the deli section, and I had my best idea of the day!

"Sausages!" I said as I pointed to a big string of sausages hanging from the ceiling.

"Yeah!" said Stew. "Gus loves sausages!"

So we bought the Cheezos, the cookies, and the sausages. And we still had some change left. We grabbed the shopping bags and rode home.

When it got dark, Stew came over to my house. He saluted me when I opened the door. He was dressed all in black. "Special Ops Agent Stew reporting for Operation Gus Grub."

I started laughing.

"We better get moving, Sergeant. Looks like there's a storm a-brewin'," he added.

I leaned out the door and could see
the wind blowing the trees around. I ran
to my room and got dressed in all black,
too. I even found some black hats for us.
Mine was a winter hat, and Stew's was a
baseball cap. We grabbed the food and
headed for Gus's.

"People can still see our faces," said Stew.

"Yeah. Special Ops guys have that black stuff to cover them up," I said.

We looked around, and then I got down on my knees and started rubbing my face on a tire of my dad's car. I looked in his side-view mirror. It was perfect.

"Soldier!" I said to Stew. "Drop and get some of this tire junk on your face!"

"Yessir!" said Stew. Then he rubbed his face on the tire. He looked awesome, and we were ready to be all stealthy and bring Gus his food.

We went over there quietly. We hid behind trees, and when it seemed that no one was looking, we'd run and roll to the next tree. We did this the whole way.

I rolled on the cookies but missed the Cheezos. I don't think anyone would have heard us anyway, because the wind was getting really loud.

When we got to Gus's house, we realized that we had no clue how to let him know we were outside.

I called up to him in a loud whisper, "Gus! Gus!" He didn't hear me because of the wind. So I threw a rock up to his window. But his window was already open.

Then Gus stuck his head out the window. "Hey!" he said quietly. "Did you bring the food?"

"Affirmative, soldier," I whispered.

Gus was like, "What?"

"I said, 'Affirmative'!" I shout-whispered.

Gus was like, "What?" again.

I just shouted:

The front-door light turned on. The door opened, and his mom looked left and right. We hid behind a bush.

The wind blew a tree branch against the house, and she looked over at that. Then she went inside.

"Yikes!" I said. "Close call."

For a few minutes, nothing happened. Gus leaned out the window. He had a toy fishing rod. He lowered the string. He had tied a big clip to it. We clipped it to the bag of Cheezos. He started reeling it up.

It was working fine, but the bag blew around and got caught on the end of the little roof under his window and ripped.

"Oh, man!" whisper-screamed Gus.
The Cheezos went blowing all over.

Stew and I opened our mouths and
tried to catch them like snowflakes. But
the Cheezos were bigger and heavier than
snowflakes. One hit me in the eye, and
Stew got one stuck in his ear. He took off
his hat to catch some Cheezos in it.

"Soldier!" I said. "Don't blow our cover! Stay in uniform!" We both started laughing at this. The wind was so strong now that the Cheezos were flying down the street.

Gus lowered the fishing line again, and we clipped the bag of Chips-a-Plenty to it. It was much heavier than the Cheezos. We could see the toy fishing rod bending. Gus started reeling it in and almost got it up to his window.

The string broke, and the cookies fell to the small roof. Gus vanished into his room and came back with one of those robot-arm toys with a grabber claw.

He reached out his window and
snatched the bag, but it slipped from the
grabber claw and fell into a tree. Then we
couldn't see it anymore.

The wind was really blowing hard now.

"How are we going to get the sausages
up to him? That's all we have left," said
Stew. Then I had my best idea of the day.

"Soldier!" I said. "You stay here and
protect our position. I will return with
reinforcements!"

"Yessir!" said Stew.

I ran home as fast as I could and back
to Gus's house.

Stew was like, "Did you bring reinforcements?"

"Negative!" I whispered. "But I brought my remote-control helicopter! We're going to airlift the sausages to the prisoner."

We hung the sausages on the bottom of the helicopter, and then we turned it on. I throttled forward, and it slowly started to rise. The sausages were pretty heavy.

"I don't know if it's gonna make it," said Stew.

"Have faith, soldier! I won't have any Negative Nancys in my ranks!"

"Yessir!" said Stew.

I started doing my military helicopter
pilot talk.

"Alpha, Bravo, Tango. Alpha, Bravo,
Tango! This is Apache One-Niner.
Permission to enter enemy airspace?"

Stew was good at military talk, too,
so he said, "This is Alpha, Bravo, Tango.
Permission granted, Apache One-Niner.
Good luck and God bless."

The helicopter slowly lifted the
sausages to Gus's window.

"Alpha, Bravo, Tango! Operation Sky Sausage is commencing," I said.

The wind started blowing the little helicopter all over. It was hard to get it to go toward the window.

"Apache One-Niner!" said Stew. "It looks like you've hit some nasty turbulence. Proceed with caution."

"Roger!" I said.

Gus looked out the window. "Oh! Yes!" he said when he saw the string of sausages. He reached the grabber claw out the window. "Come to Papa," he said.

The front door to Gus's house opened again. His mom stepped out and looked around.

"Bogey spotted!" I whisper-shouted.

The wind went crazy. Stuff was blowing everywhere. The Cheezos were twirling through the air, and the bag of cookies blew from the tree and dropped right into my face. I lost control of the helicopter. It was spinning wildly. The wind picked it up, and it went sailing into some telephone wires. Then that big box on the telephone wires began sparking and blew up like in a movie.

All of the lights on the street went out.

Stew and I froze and looked at each other for a second. Then I found the sausages on the ground. They must have been right in the explosion because they were kind of cooked.

I swung the string of smoking sausages above my head. It picked up some speed, and then I let it fly! It went right into Gus's window. It was a one-in-a-million shot!

BULL'S-EYE!

"And that's why we're dressed like Special Ops," said Ricky.

"You mean *you* blew up the transformer?" asked Ricky's dad as he pointed to the big box on the power lines.

"Yeah," said Ricky. He looked down sadly. He noticed his dad was carrying a shopping bag.

"Dad?" asked Ricky. "Why are you here, and what's in that bag?"

The front door to Gus's house opened again, and Gus's mom looked out. Ricky, Stew, and Ricky's dad hid behind a bush. As they were crouching, Ricky peeked in the bag. There were some chips, cookies, and a big salami.

"Who's all this food for?" asked Ricky, but his dad didn't answer. Gus's mom closed the door and went back in the house.

All of a sudden, Ricky's dad stood and tossed the salami up into an open window in Gus's house.

"Gus's dad is sick, too!" said Ricky's dad.

RICKY'S
ARCHAEOLOGY

#2: My Old Backpack

I haven't seen this one in years. It's from third grade. By carefully excavating the contents of the backpack, I will look back at that year of my life.

#1: Empty water bottle

#2: Once wet, but now dry and wrinkled, math workbook

#3: Three inches of worksheets and handouts from cleaning out my desk, all stuck together into one pile

#4: Once wet, but now dry and falling apart, papier-mâché dog

#5: One glove missing two fingers

#6: A flattened toilet paper tube with "DYNAMITE!" written on it

#7: Nine pieces of rock-hard gum stuck together in the shape of the United States

#8: Full, unopened lunch box believed to have been lost on field trip

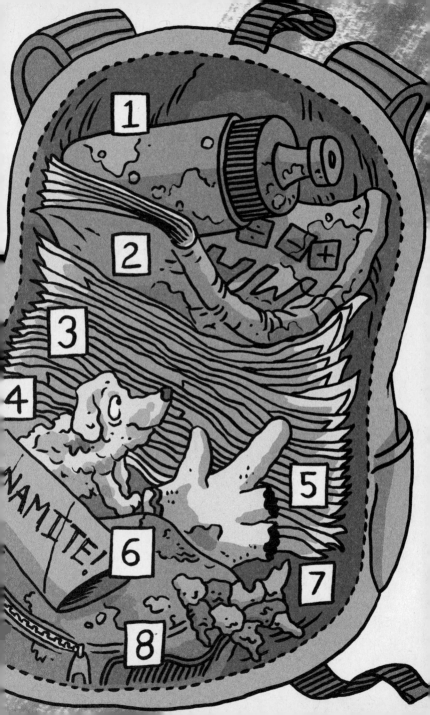

"What the heck are you doing in my chicken coop, son? And where are your pants?" asked the farmer.

"I lost my pants in the big barn!" said Ricky as he picked chicken feathers off his face.

"Why the heck were you in the barn?" asked the farmer as he leaned over his shovel.

"Because I'm the world's ugliest pig," said Ricky.

"Son, I think you left your brain in your pants, because you're making less sense than a pig frying bacon," said the farmer.

Ricky said, "Let me explain. . . ."

It all started when our class came to the farm for a writing lesson. Our English teacher, Mrs. Anderson, wanted us to describe everything we saw at the farm with as much detail as we could, using all of the five senses. Gus and I were working together. At first we were kind of goofing off. Like, instead of saying "The barn smells old and musty" or something, we would just say "The barn smells barnish" and "The tractor looks tractorish" and "The cows sound cowish" and "The goat feels goatish." We hadn't tasted anything yet.

Anyway, at one point, I put our work down to tie my shoe, and the papers were blown away by the wind. They went sailing through the air and landed in the pigpen.

I was like, "Yikes! Mrs. Anderson's gonna be mad if we don't finish the project! We have to get those papers!"

The rest of the class moved onto the field where the horses were. We hid behind the corner of the barn so we could go back to the pigpen. When we got there, we didn't see our papers.

"Where are they?" I said.

"There," said Gus. He pointed to the center of the pen, where the biggest pig was hanging out.

I looked around the farm to see if anyone else was watching. I saw some kids with their parents and another group of schoolkids, but no one was looking at the pig.

"You stand guard," I said to Gus. "Tell me if anyone is coming!" I hopped over the fence and ran to where the papers were. It was hard to run because it was so muddy, and one of my shoes came off.

SQUISH!

SQUISH!

"Someone's coming!" said Gus.

A mom and her kid came around the corner to look at the pigs. I didn't want them to see me, so I ducked into the little barn that the pigs sleep in. But it had a window and people could still see me, so I got down on the ground.

All of a sudden, these little piglets came up to me and rubbed their noses on my belly! They were climbing all over and oinking and stuff. One started sucking on my finger. They wanted me to give them milk. One got under my shirt, and it really tickled a lot. I started laughing.

Gus stuck his head through the window and whispered, "What are you doing in here?"

"Hiding!" I was still laughing from the tickling.

HA! HA!

"What's so funny?" said Gus. Then he looked left and right to make sure that no one saw him talking to a window in a pig shed, which I guess would be pretty weird.

"The pigs think I'm their mommy! They want me to give them milk!" I told him.

"That's impossible," said Gus.

"Tell *them* that!" I said.

"Hey, piggies," said Gus. "That's not your mommy. It's a dude named Ricky."

I was really laughing now.

"Hold on," said Gus, and he left the window for a second.

"I just checked, and there's no one around. Go get them," he said.

I crawled out from the pile of piglets and saw the papers sitting in the mud. They were right next to the biggest pig in the whole world. I ran as fast as I could through the squishy mud. The big pig sat down next to the papers.

I said, "No, no, no, don't!"

And then it rolled over the papers but left a corner sticking out. I pulled on the paper a bit, but I was going to rip it if the pig didn't get up. I pushed the pig hard, but it was just too big to move.

I tried to tickle the pig to see if it would get up, but it just rolled on its back, smushing the papers into the mud. I think the pig liked me rubbing it, and it fell asleep.

"Hey," called Gus, and I looked over at him. He was pointing down one of the paths around the pigpen. A small group of preschoolers was coming. I ran back into the barn area. Gus stuck his head in the window.

"Do you have them?" asked Gus.

"No. They are under that mega-pig. I can't make it move."

"How does it feel?" asked Gus.

"The mega-pig feels mega-piggish," I said, and we started laughing again.

Then I had my best idea of the day. I took some change out of my pocket and gave it to Gus. "Go get some food to feed the pig!"

Gus took the money in his hands. "The coins feel coinish."

I laughed. I watched out the window as he ran to the machine that was made for gum balls but has farm food in it, and he bought a handful. Then he ran to the other side of the shed and stood as close to the pig as possible.

I could hear him saying, "Here, piggy, piggy, piggy." The group of preschool kids gathered around him to watch. The mega-pig finally got up and walked to the fence. I could see the papers. I had to get them now, even though the kids would see me. I ran across the mud and grabbed the papers. The kids all looked up at me and screamed!

"Wow! What an ugly pig!" said Gus, and the kids started laughing. Gus is really good with little kids. I shoved the papers in my pocket, and I got down on my knees and started making piggy sounds.

"Who wants to watch me feed the ugly pig?" asked Gus, and all the kids cheered. He held out the last of his farm food. His hand was all slimy from the mega-pig.

I pretended to eat the farm food, but the mega-pig shoved me over and took the food for itself. I pushed back at the pig. Then it shoved me hard, and I fell flat on my face.

"Mrs. Anderson's coming!" said Gus. I looked across the pigpen, and our class was walking down the hill from the horse field.

I stood up and ran into the shed area. This time I just kept going. I jumped over a few small walls. I landed in cow poop.

SPLOP!

I jumped into another pen, and a goat
was there! It was really small but really
mean and tried to ram me with its little
baby horns.

I climbed another wall, jumped out of
the pens, and ran toward a door. It was
locked. I couldn't get out of the barn.
I looked out the window, and my class was
still coming. I had to be out when Mrs.
Anderson got there, or I'd be busted.
I went through the barn looking for
another place to hide or a way to get out.

I saw a really tiny door, which I thought was kind of cool, so I opened that and crawled through it. My pants caught on the edge of the door and got pulled off.

I rolled down the ramp and into a chicken coop. A rooster landed on my head, and then a chicken pecked my butt. That's when you found me.

"Hmm," said the farmer. "You did all that for a school project?"

"Yeah," said Ricky. As he stood up, he pulled his pants from the little door.

"If you hurry, you can still join your class," said the farmer. He opened the coop and let Ricky out.

Ricky's class was standing around the big pigpen, all pointing and laughing at something. Ricky and Gus walked up quietly behind them.

"What's everyone laughing at?" asked Ricky.

"That big pig is chewing on someone's shoe," said a kid.

Ricky had forgotten about losing his shoe.

"I wonder how that shoe tastes?" said another kid.

Gus and Ricky looked at each other and said, "The shoe tastes shoeish!"

RICKY'S

ARCHAEOLOGY

#3: My Old Lunch Bag

Sometimes archaeology leaves us with
more questions than answers.

#1: Why did I not eat this sandwich, and why is it now gray?

#2: Is it safe to eat this rock-hard cookie?

#3: What's the difference between blackish mold and greenish mold?

#4: Why is there an old note from Mom that says "Remember to eat your vegetables!" right next to a bag of totally black carrots?

#5: How is it possible that this apple has dried out to look exactly like an old dude?

As Ricky stood talking to Stew and his mom, Stella ran out of the house.

"Stella!" said their mom. "I told you that you can't have boys over when I'm not here!"

"I didn't," said Stella. She pointed at Ricky and said, "Her name is Uglina Grossella Hotwings!"

Their mom didn't smile. "Tell me the rest," she said calmly.

"Sure," said Ricky. . . .

I was freaking out now. "Your grandma's trying to talk to us! That's why her picture fell off the wall."

"My grandma isn't trying to contact me! She's not even dead!" said Stella. "She ran a five-K last week!"

Then she shoved me again, and this time I hit the floor.

BONK!

As soon as I fell, the moaning got louder, and there was a strange bumping noise. Stella stood up, screamed, and ran off. It sounded like the moaning was coming from the basement. I pressed my ear to the floor.

I stood up and ran to the basement. Nothing, but I could still hear the moaning. Then I figured it out!

I ran outside and to the back of the
house. I pushed through some bushes and
saw that the little door that goes into the
crawl space was open. I got down on my
belly and wiggled in.

It was really dark under there. I put my
hand out, and it landed on some crickets.
The really big green and brown ones that
live under houses!

They started hopping around like mad.
I guess they alerted the other crickets,
because all of a sudden there were like a
thousand crickets bouncing all over me and
getting stuck in my wig and stuff. I put my
face down in the dirt, and it stuck to the
makeup on my face.

Then I saw Roxy, the dog from the poster. She was stuck under the house.

She was howling so someone would help her. It wasn't a ghost!

I crawled closer. Her leash was still on, and it was caught between some pieces of wood. I tried to pull the leash free, but it was stuck. I unclipped the leash, and Roxy took off! She ran out the little door really fast.

I crawled out as quickly as I could, but the crickets were going cricket crazy and bouncing all over. As soon as I stuck my head out of the crawl space, Stella pounded me with one of those big plastic Fat Bat baseball bats.

DONK!

"Stop! Stop!" I said.

"Oh! I thought you were the ghost!" she said.

"There's no ghost! The lost dog was stuck under the house, but it got away from me!" I told her.

"No ghost?" asked Stella.

"Nope," I said. "Your house is safe!"

"You are awesome!" said Stella, and she shoved me really hard on the chest. I banged against the side of the house.

"But I didn't see a dog run by," said Stella.

We looked around outside for Roxy but couldn't find her. We ran inside to get the flyer and call the Goofenhausers to tell them we saw their dog.

Roxy was sitting on the couch, chewing a pillow.

"OH NO!" said Stella.

"We must have left the door open when we came out," I said.

"Here, Roxy, Roxy!" I called.

Roxy stood up on the couch and shook the pillow hard. The stuffing started coming out and flying all over. I stepped closer to her. She put her head down and her butt up. She wanted to play. I took another step, and she jumped over the back of the couch and knocked a lamp down.

Then she grabbed a piece of wood from next to the fireplace and ran around like a lunatic. I chased her and tried to grab her, but running in a dress is hard, and I slipped and knocked over a pile of magazines. When Stella tried to grab her, Roxy ran into the kitchen.

Roxy was going so fast she slid on the tiled floor and banged into a small table. Some potatoes fell off the table. She dropped the piece of wood, grabbed a potato, and ran out the door!

"Wow! She's really fast!" I said.

I found the flyer and handed it to Stella. "You call the Goofenhausers! I'll follow Roxy!" I said, and then I ran out the door and smashed into Stew!

"You see?" said Ricky. "We were just trying to help! C'mon! We gotta find that dog!"

A car sped up the street and stopped in front of the house.

"Hi! We're the Goofenhausers," said a lady. "Did you find Roxy?"

"Yeah," said Ricky, "but she ran off that way." He pointed down the street. They could hear a dog barking.

"I hear her," said Mrs. Goofenhauser as she jumped out of her car.

"That's her bark, all right!" cried Mr. Goofenhauser.

They all ran down the street, following the bark to Ricky's house.

Ricky and Stew looked at each other.

"The hole!" they said at the same time.

They ran to the Hole-tel.

There, at the bottom, was Roxy,
happily drinking from the toilet.

A few minutes later, the Goofenhausers
had gotten Roxy from the hole. The dog
licked their faces and wagged her tail
happily. Mr. Goofenhauser looked at
Ricky and asked, "Are you the girl who
called us?"

Ricky laughed. "No. That was Stella. My name's Ricky. I'm a boy," he said, pulling off the wig.

Mr. Goofenhauser laughed and sighed. "Well, that's a relief," he said, "because you are one really ugly girl!"